THERE'S A NIGHTMARE IN MY CLOSET

written and illustrated by Mercer Mayer

Dial Books for Young Readers | *New York*

Published by Dial Books for Young Readers
A division of Penguin Young Readers Group
345 Hudson Street • New York, New York 10014
Copyright © 1968 by Mercer Mayer • All rights reserved
Library of Congress catalog card number: 68-15250 • Manufactured in China
ISBN: 0-8037-8682-4 • ISBN: 0-8037-8683-2 (lib. bdg.)
55   57   59   60   58   56   54

Marianna

From cotton to rabbit

There used to be a nightmare in my closet.

Before going to sleep,

I always closed the closet door.

I was even afraid to turn around and look.

When I was safe in bed, I'd peek...

sometimes.

One night I decided to get rid of my nightmare
once and for all.

As soon as the room was dark, I heard
him creeping toward me.

Quickly I turned on the light and caught him
sitting at the foot of my bed.

"Go away, Nightmare, or I'll shoot you," I said.

I shot him anyway.

My nightmare began to cry.

I was mad…

but not too mad.

"Nightmare, be quiet or you'll wake
Mommy and Daddy," I said.

He wouldn't stop crying so I took
him by the hand

and tucked him in bed

and closed the closet door.

I suppose there's another nightmare in my closet, but my bed's not big enough for three.